Martha's Birthday

BRADBURY PRESS, INC. • ENGLEWOOD CLIFFS, N.J.

Martha's Birthday

Story and Pictures by
Rosemary Wells

Library of Congress Catalog Card Number:
72-104338

Manufactured in the United States of
America
First printing   13-559666-1

The text of this book is set in 16pt. Janson.
The illustrations are 3/color pre-separated
line and wash drawings.

U. S. **1903401**

FOR $\mathscr{S}.\ \mathscr{J}.$

Martha opened her birthday present from
Aunt Elizabeth.
Inside was a large pair of argyle socks.

"How nice!" said Martha's mother.
"She must have made them herself."

"Now," said Martha's mother, "because she's
    such a sweet old lady, and went to so much trouble,
    I want you to take her this pie. And wear the socks
    over to her house to show her how much you like them."
"But I hate them," said Martha.
"Don't you dare tell her that!" said Martha's mother.

Martha waited for the bus that went to
Aunt Elizabeth's house.
There was Mr. Hurdle, the grocer, sitting on the bench.
Martha stood behind a tree.
The pie leaked a little.

When the bus came Martha thought,
"Should I sit in the back and walk
   by all the people in these socks, or
   should I sit in front and hope
   that not too many people get on and
   notice them? . . . Oh why do I have such
   big feet?" she moaned.

Martha found a very fortunate seat
with a piece of newspaper on it.
"Now, should I wrap the pie in the
paper—or my feet?" she asked herself,
and then she thought, "Why do I always
have to make such horrible choices?"

Martha decided to put her coat over the socks
and forget about the paper.
An old lady got on the bus. She passed Martha
and stopped. "Coat's on the floor, dearie," she said.
"Warming," said Martha quickly.

"Oh!" said the old lady. "Do you have
  a cold? Where's your mother?"
"Home," said Martha.
"Well," said the old lady, sitting down,
"we'll just put that coat around your
  shoulders like this. . . . Why, what nice
  warm socks! How could your feet be cold in them?"
  Martha said nothing.
"Is that a pie, by any chance?"
  asked the old lady.
"Cherry," said Martha.

Martha got off the bus at the
next stop. She decided to walk
the rest of the way.
"Be careful now," called the old lady.
"I will," said Martha.

Martha found herself near a
playing field. There were some
kids she didn't know playing baseball.
One boy looked at her socks out of
the corner of his eye.
"I'd better go through the woods,"
thought Martha.

The woods were very prickly.
Brambles caught at Martha's dress
and scratched her legs.

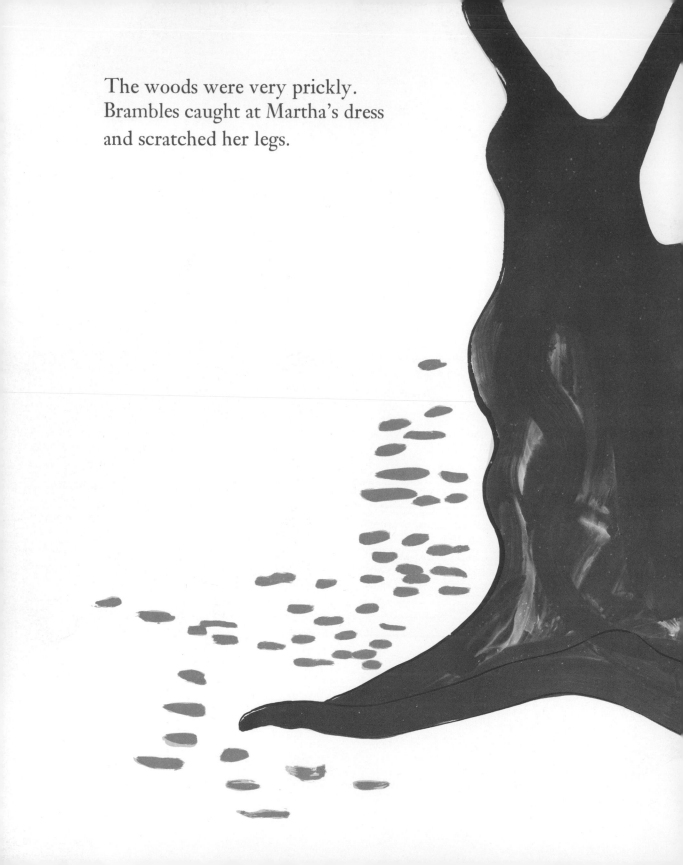

When she came to the edge of the
woods and was just in sight of Aunt
Elizabeth's house, a large German
shepherd appeared.
He looked very scary.
Martha put down the pie for him.

But he only licked it a few times and
trotted away.

"Terrible terrible terrible—
stupid stupid!"
said Martha to herself.
"Now I have to give
Aunt Elizabeth the pie
with germs on it
and she'll get sick
and it will be my fault."

Martha left the pie in the woods.
Most of it had slipped out anyway.
She walked slowly up to Aunt Elizabeth's door.
"If she gives me a bath, I'll
just die," thought Martha.

"Oh dear!" said Aunt Elizabeth,
opening the door. "You poor thing!
I made a terrible mistake. Those socks
were for your father!"

Martha didn't know whether to laugh or cry.
"Here, I have a better birthday present
for you," said Aunt Elizabeth.

Martha rode home very happy with her baby skunk.